GET A CLUE ②

25 MORE PICTURE MYSTERIES

By Lawrence Treat

Illustrated by Paul Karasik

Cover illustrations by Mary Bono

Grosset & Dunlap • New York

CONTENTS

INTRODUCTION

As everybody knows, no two things or people are exactly alike. They can come close, but never exactly. And this fact, very simply, is the key to *Get a Clue*. Still, finding the difference between two things, and the difference that that difference makes, isn't always easy.

Each puzzle in this book poses a mystery for you to solve—a mystery based on two pictures with a difference for you to spot. The best advice I can give you is to look carefully. There is always a difference, maybe several. And there is always a logical explanation for everything you see, or maybe fail to see.

Like any good detective, your job will be to build a case based on the evidence before you. Good luck. And remember, like any good puzzle-solver, you can always check your answers in the back of the book.

Lawrence Treat

A WINTER'S TALE

Julia and Julius Sneezer were excited. Their old friends, the Coughers, were coming for brunch. But an unusually cold night had left large patches of ice on their porch, making entry to their house hazardous.

Drawing **A** shows the Sneezers discussing what to do about the icy patches. Chopping the ice would damage the porch. Salting would damage

the plants. And sanding would bring dirt into the house. Suddenly their son Stevie had a bright idea.

Drawing **B** shows the Sneezers twenty minutes later, congratulating Stevie on finding a solution.

What had Stevie done?

FOUL PLAY

Pimmy Lord was the fastest runner and the best jumper in class, and he knew it. Drawing **A** shows Pimmy at Games Day, taking a breather after winning every race so far that morning: the 100-yard dash, the triple jump, and the high jump, for which he had set a new school record. "Wake me up when they announce the next event that I have to win," he said.

Drawing **B** shows the same scene a little while later, just as the next race was about to begin. "Shouldn't we wake Pimmy?" Jake Jasper asked his friend, Mike Marsh.

"Nah," said Mike. "Besides, even if we did, there's no way he could win this race." Why not?

PET SNAKE

Penelope Penrod was a budding herpetologist (a student of reptiles), who had begged her mom for years for her very own pet snake. So when Penelope found a garter snake in the garden behind her house, she wanted to keep it. But her mother objected.

Drawing **A** shows Penelope with the snake in her room before her mother walked in, screamed, and ordered Penelope to put the snake back where she found it.

Drawing **B** shows Penelope's room a little later, after she had left and her mother peeked in to inspect. Did Penelope obey her mother?

KITTY BITTIES

When Catsup, the cat, wasn't fed on time, she let everybody know it.

"Okay, okay," Frankie said, getting up from his homework and taking a can of cat food from the kitchen cabinet. "Looks like Mom bought you a brand-new brand."

Drawing **A** shows Frankie offering the new "Kitty Bitties" to Catsup, to which she gave one sniff, then turned up her nose.

"Too bad if you don't like it," Frankie said, leaving the room. "That's all you get, so you better stop bugging me."

Drawing **B** shows Frankie returning several minutes later to find Catsup's bowl still full, but the cat sleeping soundly.

How come?

BIG BLUE

The fishing tournament at Blueville-on-the-Sea attracts contestants from all over the world. Drawing **A** shows Hugh Gohunk, a Blueville native and professional fisherman, stopping to give a bit of advice to Si Blye, a new entrant. "No one ever caught anything to speak of here in Smuggler's Cove," Gohunk told him. "The best place to fish is about a mile down the shore."

Drawing **B** shows Gohunk returning a few hours later, surprised to see Blye in the same spot with a thirty-something-pounder, sure to be the grand-prize winner.

"I know you didn't catch that fish here!" Gohunk said.

Blye tried not to lose his temper. "Really? Can you prove that?" he asked. Well, can he?

SPECIAL DELIVERY

Ever since Julia and Sophia had gone to different colleges, the two sisters had written each other every week. Now that they were mothers with families of their own, they continued to correspond.

Julia had been ill, however, and had missed a week. Now her sister had gotten the same flu bug, and Julia was advising her on how to treat the illness.

Drawing **A** shows Julia beginning to write Sophia with her remedy, while her son, Miguel, looks on.

Drawing **B** shows Aunt Sophia reading the letter a few days later. Should she follow its advice?

HOME, SWEET HOME

When Mr. and Mrs. Farango and their daughter, Lia Lynn, went to Florida on vacation, they gave their housekeeper, Mrs. Morgan, a key to the house and asked her to come every day to water the plants.

Drawing **A** shows the Farango's living room as it was when they left in their usual last-minute hurry. They forgot a few things, like Mrs. Farango's camera and Mr. Farango's gum, but at least they had their airline tickets.

Drawing **B** shows the same scene as it was when the Farangos returned and found the plants well cared for. Lia Lynn, however, who had a photographic memory and a cynical mind, soon grew concerned.

Had Mrs. Morgan been a reliable caretaker?

KNIGHT FALL

Count Ossipi van Titlenot received a surprise package one day—a breastplate and a helmet from his ancestral home in Gloomst. His son, Clive, was overjoyed, because his class was studying the Middle Ages and here were two genuine pieces of armor to show.

"Oh, no!" his father said in Drawing **A**. "This is far too valuable to take to school."

Drawing **B** shows the Count and Clive coming down the next day to find that the showpieces had somehow fallen and that the helmet was badly dented.

"How did this happen?" the Count cried out.

How did it?

HOMETOWN HERO

Lefty Lefkowitz was the greatest ballplayer ever to graduate from Mockville Junior High. After his sensational high school career, Lefty went straight to a pro team, but he never forgot where he got his start. He came back after his rookie year to present his alma mater with some memorabilia: his jersey, a ball, his glove, and the bat he used in the World Series, all bearing his signature.

Drawing **A** shows him placing the items in the school's trophy case. Drawing **B** shows him one year later, back for another visit, when he stopped cold in front of the trophy case.

Why?

LOCK AND KEY

Every year, Mr. Manley took his fifth-grade class on a trip to Washington, D.C., which was paid for by the class through cookie sales, raffles, and a gala yard sale. This year, the yard sale alone had pulled in four hundred dollars, which Mr. Manley decided to keep in a locked steel box until he could take it to the bank the next day.

Drawing **A** shows him putting the box in his desk as three of his students, Shirley Hammond, Cocky Bull, and Emma Ripon, look on.

Drawing **B** shows him taking the box out the next morning, only to find that it had been pried open and the contents taken. Who took the money?

BED AND BREAKFAST—FOR FREE

The Pilchards had a small summer cottage at the beach, which they hated to leave in the autumn. Drawing **A** shows them closing it up in September. Drawing **B** shows them returning nine months later, shocked to discover that someone had been using their cottage all winter without their permission. The only clue left behind, aside from the rumpled bed and dirty dishes, was a monogrammed handkerchief on the bedside stand.

When the police were called, they came up with two suspects who had been seen wandering in the vicinity: Noah Downcast, a homeless man, and Libby Zimmelman, a teenage runaway from Ohio.

Young Marietta Pilchard soon guessed who the guilty party was. Whom did she accuse, and why?

A BEDTIME STORY

Kurt's mother was not happy when she looked in on him late Monday night in Drawing **A**. "You know it's lights-out at eight o'clock on school nights," she told him. "Get to sleep. Now!"

I guess there's no point in asking her if I can go to the SkateBoys

Club meeting tomorrow night at eight thirty, Kurt thought to himself. He knew she'd never say yes. And yet he had to go....

Drawing **B** shows Kurt the next night, all tucked in and ready for inspection at eight o'clock sharp. "Good boy," said his mother.
But is he?

FOUR-STAR RESTAURANT

Unfortunately, Janet was better at jigsaw puzzles than hockey. So to cheer her up after she failed to make the hockey team, her parents took her out to the best restaurant in town. Drawing **A** shows the waiter about to serve Janet her order of steak, when to everyone's horror he tripped on the carpet and fell.

By way of apology, the whole party was given appetizers on the house,
while a duplicate dinner was prepared for Janet. It arrived promptly,
as seen in Drawing **B**, and to everyone's satisfaction except Janet's.
Why did she object?

NO GIRLS ALLOWED

Spike and his friends were excited. They had completed their tree house using scavenged materials from town. The lumber had come from a theater that was being renovated, the windows from an old house that was being remodeled, and several old chairs had been donated by the school janitor.

Drawing **A** shows Spike's friends going home for lunch, leaving Spike to put up the "No Girls Allowed" sign by himself.

Drawing **B** shows the gang returning after a couple of hours to find the "No" crossed out and some girls making themselves at home.

"You girls changed the sign!" Butch cried.

"We did not," said Brenda. "It was like that when we got here."

Who changed the sign?

CARAMEL CUSTARD

Nathaniel hated lentils, which he regarded as a poor substitute for French fries.

"But they're good for you," his mother told him, "and if you don't clean your plate, you won't get any dessert."

Drawing **A** shows Nathaniel staring at his plate of lentils while his

mother went into the kitchen to check on his favorite dessert, caramel custard.

Drawing **B** shows him minutes later, as his mother came back. "Well, your plate is certainly clean," she said, "but I'm afraid you're still not getting any dessert."

Why did his mother deprive him?

PHONEY SCHOLAR

Sammy Richards loved to talk on the phone. As soon as he got home from school, he'd call up one of his friends, whom he had seen twenty minutes earlier, to find out what was new. If only, his parents thought, he had half as much interest in his schoolwork. And, although he begged, they refused to let him have his own phone in his room.

Drawing **A** shows Sammy's parents on their way to a town meeting. They instructed Sammy to stay off the phone and do his science homework.

Drawing **B** shows them checking in on him when they returned. "Did you do your homework?" his mother asked.

Did he?

DOG WALKER

Sylvester made his spending money by walking fancy dogs for owners who were too busy to do it themselves. While he went into each apartment building to pick up another dog, he left the rest with the doorman for safe-keeping. By the time he reached the end of the block, Sylvester would have a pack of dogs and would head into the park.

Drawing **A** shows Sylvester going in for his final pickup, Mrs. Van Doosendorf IV's spoiled spaniel, Spanky. Drawing **B** shows Sylvester returning. But instead of heading for the park, Sylvester headed for the police station. Why?

FINAL EXAM

Every Friday, Otto would meet his dad, a college history professor, at his office and they would grab a snack at the Student Union. Drawing **A** shows Otto walking in as his dad finished writing a final exam to be given the next day. Drawing **B** shows them returning after lunch, an hour later. They were surprised to find the door ajar, indicating that someone had

come in, and had possibly had a chance to examine the exam. If so, it would mean Otto's dad would have to rewrite it.

After looking around the room, Otto broke the bad news to his father. "Someone was definitely here and knows what's on that exam."

How did Otto know?

CANDLELIGHT SONATA

Melville had been taking piano lessons for three years and he still played like a beginner. This week, his teacher had given him a new piece, a simplified version of Beethoven's "Moonlight Sonata," and his mother had suggested that he practice at night. "Maybe the moonlight and candles will inspire you," she said. "Practice until they burn all the way down."

Drawing **A** shows Melville after his mother left him. Drawing **B** shows her returning later to find Melville watching TV. "I played until the candles burned down, Mom," Melville told her.

"But I've only been gone fifteen minutes," his mother said.

Did Melville follow his mother's instructions?

THE OLD SWIMMING HOLE

Judy and Jonah were two years apart. But oh, what a difference those two years made! When they were younger, they did everything together. But now Judy was growing up faster, and Jonah was having a hard time catching up.

Drawing **A** shows Judy ordering Jonah out of her room because she and her friends were about to discuss something important; in this case, where to go that afternoon, without Jonah.

Drawing **B** shows the girls after they had decided to set off for the old swimming hole and were preparing to leave. Imagine their surprise when, not long after they arrived, who should show up but Jonah. How had he known their plans?

A MATCHLESS TALE

Four deCamps, each of them weighed down with camping gear, trudged to the top of Mount Klodhopton. They reached it at noon, unpacked their supplies, and built a campfire. Then tragedy struck. No matches!

"How can we roast hot dogs without matches?" the three young deCamps asked their mom, as shown in Drawing **A**.

"I guess the matches are still in the car," Mom said with a sigh. "I'll go back and get them." And back she went.

Drawing **B** shows her returning a half hour later to find a hot dog waiting for her, cooked to perfection. "We couldn't wait, Mom," Millie said. "Figure out how we started the fire, and we'll give you a marshmallow."

"And we didn't rub two sticks together," Milton said. "The answer is right in front of your eyes."

Can you help Mom win her marshmallow?

TO BEACH A BOAT

The deKorns came from Kansas and knew nothing about the ocean. Nevertheless, they rented a seashore cottage for the month of August. It came with a rowboat, and they entrusted their son, Adam, with the care of the boat, and their daughter, Samantha, with the care of the oars.

Drawing **A** shows Adam pulling the boat out of the water at the end

of the day. Drawing **B** shows the scene the next morning, when the family discovered that the boat had disappeared.

"Adam must not have pulled the boat up high enough," his father said, "and the high tide came in during the night and carried it away."

"But Dad," Samantha said, "I don't think it was Adam's fault."

Was she right?

FATHER KNOWS BEST

Every morning at seven forty-five, seven times a week, and fifty-two weeks a year, Dennis sat at the same place at the breakfast table and listened to his father give him advice.

Drawing **A** shows Dennis listening as usual before his dad got up and left the room to get the morning paper and a cup of coffee. Today,

his father's advice dealt with it being the first of the month. "A good time,"
Dennis's father said, "for taking advantage of opportunities."

Drawing **B** shows his father back at the table ready to continue his sermon,
and Dennis trying to stifle a laugh.

Why?

THE LEMONADE STAND

Binky and Becky hoped to make a tidy profit selling lemonade on a
hot summer day in August, until their first customer informed them that
their lemonade was too sour.

Drawing **A** shows Becky going inside to get more sugar. "I'll be back in a minute. Just don't drink up the profits, Binky!" she said.

Drawing **B** shows Becky upon her return. Why does she look so mad?

ANSWERS

A WINTER'S TALE (pages 6-7)

Stevie took the iron and ironed the ice off the porch. Problem solved. But on leaving home, Frank Cougher slipped on the ice on *his* porch and sprained his ankle. Perhaps the brunch was never meant to be.

FOUL PLAY (pages 8-9)

Pimmy would have little chance of making it to the starting line in time after having to stop and untie the knots that had been tied in his shoelaces by his fellow athletes.

When Pimmy woke up, he thought it not funny.

The other boys thought it knot funny.

What about you?

PET SNAKE (pages 10-11)

No, as her mother deduced when she spotted the new air holes in the box on the bookshelf. Rather than punish Penelope, however, Mrs. Penrod realized that her daughter had a true and deep love for living things, including snakes, and that it was a love to be encouraged. She not only let Penelope keep her new pet, but bought her a book on herpetology and a large, secure glass case in which to keep the snake. But Mrs. Penrod still hated snakes!

KITTY BITTIES (pages 12-13)

The Kitty Bitties were untouched, but that didn't mean that Catsup hadn't eaten. The droplets of water by the fish tank and the two missing fish in Drawing **B** show that Catsup had dined, à la carte, on goldfish.

BIG BLUE (pages 14-15)

Yes, Gohunk can prove that Blye did not catch that fish. Gohunk noticed that the spider web on Blye's rod in Drawing **A** had not been broken, as it would have been if Blye had used it.

Detailed investigation proved that Blye had bought the fish a day before and kept it alive until the morning, when he put it in his cooler, hauled it out in the privacy of Smuggler's Cove, and pretended that he had caught it.

Shortly after the discovery of the fraud, Blye disappeared mysteriously and has not been seen since. Neither has the spider.

SPECIAL DELIVERY (pages 16-17)

Yes and no.

Yes, the flu remedy is at least worth a try.

The postscript, however, is not Julia's best advice, because Julia didn't write it. The handwriting in the main body of the letter contains no loops, whereas the handwriting in the postscript, which Miguel quickly added while his mother was looking for an envelope, has distinct loops.

Aunt Sophia was not about to forget her nephew's birthday. But now, instead of cash, she sent him a box of stationery.

HOME, SWEET HOME (pages 18-19)

No. Lia Lynn noticed that one of the numbers on their five-hundred-dollar lottery ticket was different than it had been when they left. She had memorized those numbers especially because her father had promised to buy her a TV if they won.

Once she noticed the change, she asked herself why, and decided that the only explanation could be that the original ticket had won and had been stolen and replaced. And she was right.

As a result, Lia Lynn got her own TV, and Mrs. Morgan had to return the lottery winnings. At 8 percent interest.

KNIGHT FALL (pages 20-21)

The Count's fancy for medieval artifacts got the better of him and impelled him to sneak downstairs during the night and try on the breastplate and helmet. To his surprise, it felt so good, he took a walk and was having a fine time imagining himself back in time a thousand years until the helmet dropped down over his eyes, causing him to trip and fall down the stone stairs, denting the helmet, breaking a stone step, and leaving the count with a small abrasion on the top of his bald head. The Count covered it with a bandage and pushed the armor stand over to make it look as if something had come in and knocked it down. But young Clive hadn't been born yesterday, you know!

HOMETOWN HERO (pages 22-23)

Lefty was a lefty. And as everyone knows, left-handed baseball players throw with their left hand and catch with their right. In Drawing **A**, Lefty is placing his own right-hand glove in the display case. In Drawing **B**, a left-hand glove is in its place.

When the thief was caught, he denied his guilt, but there was no denying that though Lefty was a lefty, in this case, he was right.

LOCK AND KEY (pages 24-25)

Mr. Manley. He had the only key to the strongbox and used it to get the box open. Then, in order to cast suspicion elsewhere, he jimmied open the side of the box with a screwdriver to make it look as though someone had opened it by force. But his mistake was in putting the lock back on with the logo, AJAX, no longer in view.

When the class left for Washington, Mr. Manley waved them good-bye.

BED AND BREAKFAST—FOR FREE (pages 26-27)

Marietta accused Libby, although her father said the handkerchief's was Noah's because it had an 'N' on it.

"But Dad," Marietta said, "hold it the other way, and it's a 'Z'—for Zimmelman. And only a kid would pick the top bunk to sleep in."

A BEDTIME STORY (pages 28-29)

No. Kurt had a plan: To go to bed with his clothes on, then sneak out of his window after his mother said good night and go to the SkateBoys meeting, as planned, which is why his pajamas are hanging in his closet in Drawing **B**, and why his sneakers are not there.

And his plan worked. Perfectly. Until Kurt came home and realized that he couldn't climb back into his room. The window was too high. So he had to ring the doorbell.

The moral of this story: A good general plans his retreat as well as his attack.

FOUR-STAR RESTAURANT (pages 30-31)

Janet's sharp eyes noticed that the steak was exactly the same shape as the piece that the waiter had dropped, just flipped over.

Janet's mother and father toasted Janet, as well as the maitre d', who oversaw the preparation of another steak and served it free of charge. But what Janet really wanted was to play on the hockey team.

The next year, she did.

NO GIRLS ALLOWED (pages 32-33)

Spike crossed out the word "No" while the sign was still upside-down on the ground, before he even nailed it and left for lunch. If the word "No" had been painted over after it had been hung, the wet paint would have dribbled down from the line in the opposite direction, toward the ground.

Spike secretly wanted girls in the club. He thought they would be fun, and he was right. They contributed a slide, a tire swing, and a rope ladder.

Nobody ever figured out that it was Spike who crossed out the word "No," and after a while, nobody cared.

CARAMEL CUSTARD (pages 34-35)

Nathaniel's plate was too clean, and the flower pot next to him was too full. His mother figured out that he had dumped his lentils into the flower pot, where he hoped they would not be noticed.

No dessert was his just deserts.

PHONEY SCHOLAR (pages 36-37)

Sammy never used the phone, but he didn't do his homework either. The science book remains open to the same page it was when his parents left. The novel on his nightstand, however, has been read, as indicated by the different placement of the bookmark.

Sammy got a D in science, but with his combination of a love of reading and talking, he became a famous talk show host.

DOG WALKER (pages 38-39)

Sylvester noticed that the dalmatian in the pack had different spots from the dog he had left, and suspected the doorman of stealing the valuable dalmation and substituting another.

The police caught the doorman with the pedigreed dalmatian and returned it to its rightful owners, and Sylvester got to keep the replacement.

FINAL EXAM (pages 40-41)

Otto noticed that the copier, which, in Drawing **A**, had been set to make a single copy, had been changed to make eleven copies. That meant not only had someone seen the exam but duplicates were circulating.

When Otto's father realized he had to write a new exam, he groaned.

When his students realized they had to take a different exam, they groaned.

CANDLELIGHT SONATA (pages 42-43)

Yes, he played until the candles burned down, but his mother knew that it should have taken far longer than fifteen minutes. However, the curtain caught in the closed window in Drawing **B** indicates that the window had been opened and then closed, obviously by Melville, to let the strong evening breeze blow in on the candles, making them burn down faster. The accumulation of melted wax on the left side of the candles further bears this out.

The next evening, Melville's mother put away the candelabra and brought out the kitchen timer.

THE OLD SWIMMING HOLE (pages 44-45)

In Drawing **A**, as he was being kicked out, Jonah pushed the "record" button on Judy's tape player so that everything they said was recorded. In Drawing **B**, the tape is advanced all the way, indicating that the girls' conversation has been recorded. After the girls left, Jonah returned to Judy's room, played back the tape, and discovered their plans.

And when the girls reached the swimming hole, there was Jonah.

A MATCHLESS TALE (pages 46-47)

The answer was actually in front of Milton's eyes. The kids used his glasses to concentrate the bright sunlight and set some scraps of paper ablaze. From this, they were able to build a fire and roast their hot dogs.

Mom figured this out when she noticed that the cord attached to Milton's glasses was no longer in back of his neck but in front of it. A sure sign that he had taken off his glasses.

Later on the deCamps discovered that they'd left the marshmallows at the bottom of the mountain, too.

TO BEACH A BOAT (pages 48-49)

Yes, she was. The deposit of seaweed halfway up the beach indicates the high-tide line, which Adam clearly pulled the boat past. Besides, had the tide come in and floated the boat away, the water would have washed away the marks left in the sand by the boat's keel. Instead, the groove in the sand shows that the boat was dragged away by someone after high tide had already come and gone.

Therefore, instead of reporting a missing boat, the family reported a stolen boat, which the police quickly discovered in the next cove.

Adam thanked his sister for clearing his name. "It's no big deal," she said. "But from now on, you can do all the rowing, while I do all the fishing."

FATHER KNOWS BEST (pages 50-51)

Following his father's advice, Dennis took advantage of an opportunity. When his father left the room, Dennis poured most of the salt from the salt shaker into the sugar bowl. After all, it was April Fools' Day. And when his father came back with his cup of coffee, sweetened it, and took a good long sip, he was certainly fooled.

THE LEMONADE STAND (pages 52-53)

Becky noticed not that some lemonade was gone, but that there was more than before. To hide the fact that he'd drunk half the pitcher, Binky had refilled it with water from the garden hose, as shown by the drops of water at the end of the hose in Drawing **B**.

Now, because the lemonade was too watery, Binky had to go back to get more lemons. He came back with the news—no more lemons.

ABOUT THE CREATORS

Lawrence Treat, novelist and short story writer, is a two-time recipient of the Edgar Allan Poe Award, the highest honor in the field of mystery writing. He was also a prizewinner at the Crime Writers' International Short Story Contest, held in Stockholm, Sweden, in 1981, and received a ceremonial dagger in Tokyo from the Mystery Writers of Japan. A founder and past president of the Mystery Writers of America, Mr. Treat is the originator of the picture-mystery puzzle, many of which also appear in his best-selling series *Crime and Puzzlement*. He lives on Martha's Vineyard with his wife, artist Rose Treat.

Paul Karasik has illustrated two of Mr. Treat's previous picture-mystery puzzle books. He is a former associate editor of *Raw Magazine*, the international comics review. With artist David Mazzuccelli, he adapted Paul Auster's *City of Glass* into a graphic novel that has been translated into four languages. He, too, lives on Martha's Vineyard with his family.

Drawing **A** shows Mr. Treat and Mr. Karasik beginning work on *Get a Clue*. Drawing **B** shows them with just one puzzle left to do. See if you can deduce why they almost could not finish.

Answer: A broken pen nib. Luckily, there was a pencil handy.